RIGHT SIGHT

DANIEL HILL ZAFREN

RIGHT
SIGHT

A
MURDER
MYSTERY

DANIEL HILL ZAFREN

Published by Time Treasures Books, Goose Creek, South Carolina

www.timetreasuresbooks.com

ISBN: 978-1-7345129-0-8

Cover and interior by Susan Newman Design Inc.

The earlier books by Daniel Hill Zafren:

In a World We Never Made (2001)
A Door Never Opened (2003)
Shadow Selves (2005)
Network of Death (2006)
Not Lost – Just Not Found (2008)
Restless Beauty (2009)
Glimpses of Forgotten Dreams (2010)
Echo in the Heart (2011)
Double Hugs (2011)
Page Passage (2013)
Wish Winds (2014)
Unfinished Thinking (2015)
Vain Regrets (2016)
Network Secret (2016)
Forever Old, Forever New (2017)
Endless Time (2018)
A Gray Voyager (2019)

RIGHT SIGHT

Certain sight terms are well known and defined, such as hindsight, foresight, and insight.

Hindsight is the understanding of a situation or event after it has happened.

Foresight is the ability to predict and prepare for future events and needs.

Insight is the ability to see and understand the truth about someone or something.

Right sight is much more nebulous. It can be considered a combination of the abilities of the other sight terms listed above. The degrees of each vary depending on the events, circumstances, and persons involved. It can lead to an empty and frustrating end, or it can produce a bountiful harvest of illuminating and useful results, or it can wind up anywhere in between.

ONE

If "murderfree" was a real word, the dictionary might define it as the absence of a murder. As a concocted term, it would have been an apt description of the town of Braxton located on Braxton Lake in the northern section of New York State close to the Canadian border. The two-mile town limit parallels the length of the lake. In the more than two hundred years since the town's founding there had never been a murder there, or any other serious crime for that matter. So, when the body of Julius Mauer was discovered on an early spring night on the shore of the lake with a knife in his back, it sent shock waves throughout the town. Whispers matched the eerie feeling that things would never be the same in Braxton.

The town had a nearly steady year round population of about four hundred, increased by another two hundred during the summers when the cottages on the lake were fully occupied. The town was established by Maurice Braxton after he discovered and laid claim to the lake in the early nineteenth century. He was wealthy and influential, and immediately after having his enormous house built at the northern end of the lake, a series of small houses were built down from the main house for the overflow of his house servants as well as the workers to maintain his fields and orchards. The elegant Braxton mansion has always been known as Braxton Manor.

As surrounding areas grew and aligned with the State, Maurice Braxton was able to independently incorporate the town and lake and keep it apart from the adjoining county of Whiteton which had attempted to annex it. This complete independence exists as of today so that the Sheriff of Whiteton has no jurisdiction in the town or over the lake.

The Braxton wealth still exists, although somewhat diminished by modern standards. A fifth generation daughter, Phyliss Braxton, an elderly spinster, lives in Braxton Manor with a maid, cook, and gardener. The house has been refurbished numerous times, and is still the jewel of the community. The fields and orchards have long since been grown over and in disuse, although extensive bountiful gardens were still maintained. A stable with riding horses as well as a horse drawn carriage and sleigh were kept in good condition. The original worker houses that still remain are mainly occupied by employees at the box factory in Barrington, fifteen miles to the south. Additional cottages were built around the lake after World War II when folks down state sought respite from the summer heat and were attracted to the recreation the lake offered. It is a glacier lake, picturesque, with exceptionally clean and clear water.

As with many other small towns, Braxton had in some ways seen better days. There was a time when a series of shops lined the main street offering a variety of goods and attractions. Most were vacant now, hapless victims to the large shopping mall near Barrington. A walk through town meant passing vacant store after vacant store like ghosts hovering above the street. Braxton did fare better than many other towns because of the Braxton money which was readily available for vital services and maintenance of the town, including the public beach, the picnic areas, and the boat ramps. At Christmas, Braxton Manor was open for residents to visit and partake of special foods offered for the occasion. A further positive for the town and its residents were the lakeside cottages. A number of the folks in town either owned a cottage and benefited from the summer rental fee or they offered some form of service to the summer residents, such as cleaning or maintenance. Even in the winter, people come to the lake to skate and ice fish.

Eighty-two-year-old Farrell Hollingsworth was probably the most recent inhabitant of Braxton, and that had been eighteen years ago when he retired as a homicide detective at the New York City Police Department. Considering his background, one would think that the murder would not have been a shock to him, but it was for two reasons. It was the last thing he expected to happen in Braxton. It was also the last thing he wanted to happen. Because of his background, eight years earlier when Mayor Denton thought a form of police presence should be established in the town for appearance sake, he impressed on Farrell to accept the title of Braxton Chief Law Enforcer and authorized his cottage on the lake as police headquarters. The Mayor knew he was skilled in creating miniature wooden houses, and he assured him that there would be very little interference with his time and energy. That had proven to be the case as he was rarely called on for any so-called official duties. With no traffic lights or parking meters in the town or at the public beach, an occasional traffic control need arose for a funeral, or a parade, or there might be a littering problem, or a lost dog. Now, it seemed as if he was the only one who had jurisdiction over the murder.

Farrell had started building wooden miniature houses early during his police career and it escalated during the lonely long care taking hours when his wife, Beverly, had become ill, a protracted and painful medical battle which eroded the vibrant life of a forty-two-year-old woman. That death brought to an end their twelve year marriage. With no children and no living relatives, Farrell lost himself for the next twenty years in his detective job and in constructing the miniature houses. Gradually, as he amassed a sizable inventory of his creations he gained a certain notoriety. Some of the houses sold at a good price, although when he gauged how much time and energy he put into the effort there was some doubt as to the true economic viability. His enjoyment and satisfaction with the activity was paramount, and it was still a connection to Beverly.

The long hardship of detective work with all of its accompanying horrors eventually took its toll, and without a home life to offset the harshness of the crime world he was unable to continue productively in the job. Retirement was the only solution, and between his police pension and miniature house sales he figured he could retire anywhere he wanted to. There was no family or strong social bonds holding him to New York City. Going to Florida was appealing, but it just did not seem right for him. To counter the grueling years involved with ghastly crimes and the loss of Beverly which still lingered in his heart, he coveted a quiet and nonintrusive existence. Memories as a boy when for six summers his family had rented a cottage on Braxton Lake nudged him to choose that place to settle down in. He believed he was the only person to have ever retired there.

TWO

The small cottage on the lake was all that Farrell wanted or needed. The only furniture he brought with him from the New York City apartment were the tables and lamps used for his artistic endeavor, a small sofa, a dresser, the marital bed which was more sentimental than required, a night stand, and the kitchen table and two chairs. There was no room in the cottage for anything else anyway. The bed, night stand, and dresser barely fit in the one bedroom. The work tables filled the living room, which was the largest room. The stool he used fit under one of the tables when not in use. The tools used in the process were in a special crate he had built.

The one item he did purchase shortly after moving in was a rocker placed as the only item on the small back porch. Farrell would sit in that chair for long hours, in heat or cold, staring out over the lake. A lake view was a desired change from the urban landscape of New York City. The essence of the lake was also a further connection to Beverly. There were the memorable times during their summer vacations that they would boat or canoe on a lake. He particularly liked the view of the lake early in the morning when the mist lay close to and seemed to glide over the water. It idealized how the beauty and essence of the lake cannot be seen although it is still there, reaffirmed when the mist clears. At times, it was almost as if Beverly would appear in the clearing.

An old boat wreck that was near the shoreline below his cottage when he moved in was still there even though many had complained it was an eyesore. Over the years it had gained a special symbolism for him. It meant that even things can die, and the significance of that death can continue on. So, too, it was with the death of Beverly.

Those peaceful moments would be conducive to letting his agitated spirit reach a certain calmness. Over the years, memories of the police work became less frequent and more distant. The memories of Beverly would take hold and a flicker of warmth would fill his heart and the longing would magically make those memories real and meaningful. Some loves are forever.

Farrell's favorite recall of Beverly was when they first met. He was a rookie police officer and she was, as she described herself, a Bohemian poet who went from coffee house to coffee house in Greenwich Village. She would recite her poetry to any who might listen and drop some coins in the old felt hat she wore to and from the recitals. He had a studio apartment in Greenwich Village and when he was off duty he would often stroll the quaint streets fascinated by the shops. On one such stroll, he caught a glimpse of her just as she was about to enter a coffee shop. She was probably not more than five feet tall and the floppy dress reaching to her ankles could not hide her frail frame. She had long straight brown hair and had a misshapen hat on top of her head. He figured she was fifteen years old, maybe sixteen. He entered the coffee house she had gone into and sat at one of the many empty tables. She was sitting on a stool on a raised platform reciting poetry. Her large brown eyes starred into space, and it apparently did not bother her that there were few people there and that none might be listening. Her melodic voice was mesmerizing, and he had to suppress a sudden urge to go up to her and hug her protectively. The alluring brown eyes then leveled and met his gaze, and it then seemed as if she was reciting just for him. Her look was spellbinding, riveting even in the memory of it. He had never been drawn to another person like that. When she grew silent, he was the only person in the place that applauded. Her gaze shifted to the empty felt hat turned upside down at her feet. It was as if she was saying, "If you liked it, please put some money in the hat. I haven't eaten for two days." Or, was she reaching across the room with her heart seeing at last a person who saw her without looking through her. She reached into the canvas bag slung across her shoulder and pulled out a pad and pen, opened the pad and feverishly scribbled on the page before her. When he stood up and went to her and dropped the ten dollar bill into the hat she handed him the paper she tore from the pad. He must have read that poem a thousand times, committed to his mind from that day and for all days.

Yearning can be in the eyes as well as in the heart,
>> *The message I see in your eyes is a reflection of my own;*
Emotional travels can be set smoothly from the start,
>> *Even if the destination is not fully known.*

Take care to keep secrets from prying eyes,
>> *An exercise not difficult if diligently applied;*
Rewards for the heart and mind are easy to visualize
>> *If human contact is simplified.*

Assuming the crystal ball does not lie,
>> *I await a proposal to be in your presence;*
To explore the when, where, and why
>> *Of a budding feeling and its essence.*

The dream world he was immersed in shattered when the cell phone rang. He did not have a telephone when he moved to Braxton, not really needing or wanting one. When he was made Chief Law Enforcer he was given a cell phone so that he could be contacted if necessary. He could count on one hand the times the cell phone had rung for his so-called official duties.

"Farrell, Mayor Denton here. Everyone is asking. What are you doing about the murder?"

Farrell resented being thrust back into reality, but he knew he was boxed in. "I am doing what needs to be done. The State Coroner in Albany has agreed to do the autopsy. The crime scene was sealed off with your help but has revealed little. There is one shoe print in the mud close by although it may be totally unrelated to the crime. The knife is a common one-in-million kitchen type that probably is untraceable. It was wiped clean of fingerprints or the killer was wearing gloves. I am drawing up a list of town people to interview, but you know as well as I do that Julius was the least popular person around. Unless some interstate connection arises so I can bring in the FBI on this, I am on my own. Something will break. It usually does."

"What about the possibility that the murderer is a traveler to or from Canada?"

"Remote, I think. Without an eyewitness, I need to go first and foremost that this is purely a local act."

"What about someone using the beach?"

"The beach is closed at this time of the year."

"What about one of his business contacts elsewhere?"

"That can be a big area for one person to investigate. If it is not a person from town, I'll have to go that route. That will take much time and effort. An old man may not be up to all that.

You may have to come up with someone younger to take over for me."

"You're the best we got."

"You're more sure than I am."

"Upset the apple cart, for sure. I still can't believe it. Why? Who?"

Farrell sighed. "Little big questions."

"Let me know what is going on every step of the way."

"I will let you know anything I find out."

"I am counting on you to solve this quickly and quietly so we can move on."

"I hope it works out that way."

THREE

Farrell tried to distance himself from the people of Braxton. He needed and wanted his solitude, and friendships had a way of intruding on that. His closest acquaintance was Horton Blake. Horton owned and operated the only general store and gas station in town. People in the town had no closer choice for what they needed, and the only other option was to go to the larger stores and gas stations near Barrington. Horton was the first person Farrell met when he moved there, and Horton kept a sharp eye out on and knew more about most of the people in town than anyone else. What he did not know, Greta, his wife, knew as she worked along side of him every day in the store. So, Farrell asked Horton to compile a list for him of those he thought should be interviewed about the murder. Of course, Felipe Hernandez, who discovered the body, would be interviewed first and then the list would kick in.

Horton had also been financially helpful to Farrell. Once he saw Farrell's artistic creations, he cleared out a small section of the store for display and sale of the houses. The shelving unit accommodated six houses. Horton did not charge him anything but kept twenty-five percent of any sale. Over all of the years there had only been three sales, all to people going to or coming from Canada that had stopped at the store for gas, necessities, or information. Horton liked having the houses for display as it often prompted conversation with customers and, if nothing else, people would stop and look at them and linger long enough so they might see some other items they might be interested in. Horton and Greta were neither bashful nor short on talk.

"As you wanted, Farrell," Horton said in a boastful manner, "I jotted down some folks you might want to talk to. There is nobody in town who liked Julius, but these six people had a particular animosity towards him or special knowledge about him."

The list read:

- Jane Morgan – Julius' ex-wife
- Grace Ballantree – the young widow Julius was always after for romantic involvement
- Peter Chaussen – owed Julius much money from failed loans
- David Steele – Julius' next door neighbor; lots of disagreements over the years
- Maxine Rhinegold – the town clerk who was very vocal in opposition to many of Julius' ideas to take advantage of the town
- Graciella Avello – Julius' housekeeper for many years

Farrell looked at both Horton and Greta. "Sorry, but I have to ask. Who do you think may have done it?"

Greta raised an eyebrow, a wisp of hair dangling down over her dampened forehead, "Could be anyone. He would come in here once and awhile, and was always nasty to us or any other person in here. I don't think he ever did anything good."

"I agree," Horton chimed in. "Sure do hope it turns out to be an outsider for the town's sake."

"Maybe I'll find out when I talk to them," Farrell responded. "Can you fill me in on Mauer's background?"

Horton was pensive for a moment. "Don't know much for certain. Don't know where he came from or what he did before he moved here, but he must have had some interest in the Domingo house when it went on the market some thirty years ago. He bought it, moved in, hired Graciella as a live-in housekeeper, and let it be known that he had money to lend. Graciella had lived in a small house with her brother, and made a scant living cleaning houses. Don't know how the two hooked up, and don't know how she has served the man all of these years."

"Thanks for the list. Let me know if you think of anything else that might help."

Farrell went home and sat in the rocker on the porch with the list, pondering the order he would follow after he questioned Felipe Hernandez. He took out a pen and added to the list Ava Williams, the waitress at the only diner in town, The Cup and Saucer. She very well may have heard some interesting things over the years, especially from those who sat at the counter close to where she was most of the time. He thought he would start with her and then go to the housekeeper, Graciella Avello, who might have knowledge of some of the more intimate thoughts and actions of the deceased.

He was tired, and a small voice in his mind kept telling him he was too old for such cloak and dagger activities. He could not think of a way to extricate himself from the position he was in. He also did not need the voice to tell him what was all too obvious to him – he was far too rusty in planning and carrying out a murder investigation.

Farrell closed his eyes and Beverly's daunting image appeared before him. As if he had not been interrupted, the earlier recall of his first encounter with that sweet and adorable woman continued.

Picking up the hat and stuffing Farrell's ten dollar bill in her canvas bag, she stepped off of the platform and stood before him. She barely came up to the top of his chest. A warm smile revealed perfect teeth and dimples in her cheeks. "Thank you, kind sir," the mesmerizing voice offered.

"And thank you for the poem."

"It is a rhyming invitation to get to know you. I like what I see and what I sense about you. I like what I feel and feel what I like. I am a Bohemian poet, outspoken, and unconventional."

"I am the opposite. I am an introvert, reserved, and shy to the utmost, especially with women."

"Wow!" Her exclamation sounded like a surprise although he guessed she had already figured him out. "We make the perfect pair. Since you so easily parted with the ten bucks, do you, kind sir, have any more money to buy me a hot dog from the cart down the street? I am hungry enough to eat a bear but a dog will do."

"Sure. First, tell me your name."

"Beverly Myers."

"Real name or pen name?"

"I'm as real as you get." That would be proven to him time and time again. "And you?"

"Promise you won't laugh."

"Promise."

"Farrell Hollingsworth."

She laughed anyway. "Are you as stuffy as that sounds?"

"Probably more so."

"Good. I love a challenge. First thing, I am going to call you Far and, young man, you and I are going to go far together."

She put her arm through his and they went to the hot dog

cart where she ordered a hot dog with chili, onions, relish, mustard, and sauerkraut. They went to the little park at the end of the street and he watched her consume the food in record time. Perhaps, it had been two days since she had eaten last.

That was close to the truth as they spent the next hour talking. She lived in a group home on upper Broadway, and her last meal was the day before. She had nothing, wanted nothing, and loved nothing. At least until she met him because he definitely was something. She was not fifteen or sixteen but actually twenty-five, two years older than he was. She could not believe he was a police officer, and insisted on kissing his cheek to see how tough he was. His heart had already melted, and the kiss was icing on the cake.

Farrell raised his hand now to the spot on his cheek where the kiss had lingered. It sealed his fate.

FOUR

Felipe Hernandez was a part time handyman for Phyliss Braxton. He lived with his wife, Margarita, and three small children in an old clapboard house on the edge of town near Braxton Manor. Several evenings a week he would go to the lake to fish and hopefully catch enough for a meal. On the night he found the body, since he had no cell phone he panicked and ran all the way to Mayor Denton's house. The Mayor called Farrell and the two arrived at the lake at the same time. Farrell put police tape around the crime scene and did a preliminary appraisal of the area as best as he could with a flashlight in the dark. The Mayor kept the people who flooded down to the lake upon hearing about the killing beyond the taped area. Waiting for the State Coroner to send a van to collect the body was the hardest part. Many disjointed thoughts raced through Farrell's mind. He would have to do a more thorough examination in the daylight and hope nobody ventured into the area before that to contaminate it. There did not seem to be much to be tampered with, and Farrell would have to go with whatever he found. There was really no way to tell initially whether Mauer was killed at the lake or his body was taken there after the killing.

Farrell knocked on the door to the Hernandez home. A young girl opened the door. "Is your father home?", Farrell asked.

"No, senor," the girl responded in a squeaky voice.

Margarita then appeared behind the girl. "Good day, Mr. Hollingsworth."

"Hello, Margarita. Is Felipe here?"

"No," she answered a bit tentatively.

"Do you know where he is?"

"He is working at Miss Braxton's house, on the fence, I think."

"Thanks, I'll catch up with him there."

Farrell had never been to Braxton Manor in all the years he had been there. He had never spoken to Phyliss Braxton either, although he had seen her a few times from a distance.

It was a short walk to the Braxton property. Felipe was painting the fence bordering the horse corral and Phyliss Braxton was standing besides him. She was tall and lanky with short cropped silver gray hair. He would describe her as a handsome looking woman. Her features were finely etched with straight lines and her bearing was regal. He hazarded a guess that there was not an ounce of fat on the body encased in the black pants suit. Felipe, on the other hand, was short and chubby and his overalls were smudged with dirt and streaked with paint.

"I am Farrell Hollingsworth," he announced to Miss Braxton trying to assert an air of authority.

"I know who you are," she offered in a resonant voice with perfect diction. "Have you found the killer yet?"

He snorted. "I don't believe in miracles."

Her nose twitched perceptively, "Well, you won't find him or her here."

He thought it interesting the way she phrased that remark, and he would reflect on it later. "I would like to talk with Felipe, if you don't mind. But, as long as you are here, do you know anything that might help?"

She did not respond right away, and he thought she was going to tell him to go. "No, I do not. I do not associate with the likes of Julius Mauer." Without another word she turned and walked towards the house, leaving him alone with Felipe.

Farrell could not tell whether that was just a statement of fact or a subtle invitation for him to come back and talk to her when Felipe was not around. "She is not very friendly," he said to Felipe.

Felipe relaxed noticeably and smiled. "She is O.K. It takes her time to warm up to someone. She is always good to me."

"That's nice. Tell me about finding the body."

Felipe reiterated his story about going fishing, finding the body, and then running to Mayor Denton's house. He added that he knew who Mauer was and recognized the body but had never had any dealings with him. Farrell shrugged his shoulders, thanked Felipe, and headed to the diner.

The exact age of The Cup and Saucer could not be pinpointed. Some say it was built before World War I; others say it was a product of the Depression. Whatever its age and its dingy and uninteresting facade, it was the only game in town. If one wanted a meal out in town, the diner was the only choice, and it had limited hours as well. There were six swiveling stools along a twenty foot counter and six tables with four chairs around each table. It was owned by Raymond O'Hara, a long-time summer resident, who bought it some fifteen years earlier at a bankruptcy sale. Besides the waitress, Ava Williams, there was a short order cook, Manuel Cortez.

Farrell would stop in at the diner occasionally for breakfast if he had to go to town for something. He figured it was safe to have a muffin and coffee, although he would speculate that the old coffee urn was rarely cleaned thoroughly. Whenever he was in there, there were few patrons and the only noise came from a small television that Ava watched constantly when not busy. They would make general conversation, although Ava welcomed any diversion and would always try to make him talk more even though she knew he was a private person. He guessed her to be in her late fifties, straight hair dyed a deep red, and with a pleasant face with too much makeup on in an attempt to cover deep lines probably resulting from a strenuous life and a hot kitchen. Beverly never wore any makeup, not even lipstick.

"I figured you'd be in sooner or later," Ava greeted him in a husky voice.

"Sooner it is. Is the coffee fresh?"

She grinned. "Is sliced bread sliced? Fresh is relative."

"Not a relative of mine. Let me have it in a clean cup, please."

The diner was empty. He sat on a stool. "Is the conversation fresh?"

"Depends."

"You know why I am here."

A deep sigh as she stared out the dirt streaked window. "Can't help you much. Mauer never came in here. He probably thought he was too good for a place where ordinary folks go. Never heard a kind word spoken about him either."

"Anybody say anything especially negative recently?"

"No." Her response was a bit too quick for Farrell's liking.

"Are you sure?"

"Yeah."

"What did you think about him?"

"Some twenty years ago I passed him on the street. He pinched my butt. Haven't spoken to him since."

"Did you resent what he did?"

"Surprised a bit I suppose. He has done worse to others as you probably know."

"No, I don't know. Like what?"

"Beat his wife, poor thing."

"How do you know that?"

"People talk."

"Which people?"

"You sound like a detective."

"I am a detective."

"Then you will find out all that without me naming names. I don't want a knife in my back."

He drained the last of the coffee from the cup deciding not to comment that the coffee was bitter. "I can't catch a killer without cooperation."

She feigned a laugh. "If you are depending on what I know, you are in deep doo-doo. If I was you, I'd lock up the whole town. You'd have the killer that way."

He rose. "Thanks for nothing."

"Nothing it is. The coffee is on me."

He was weary and not sure his mind would be at peak performance, but the pressure to find the killer led him to one more interview for the day. He would talk to Graciella Avello, Mauer's live-in housekeeper and also hope she would let him look through the house and at Mauer's papers.

The Mauer house was at the opposite end of town from Braxton Manor. It was larger than most of the other houses, and the imposing wrought iron fence surrounding it was intimidating and indicated that trespassing was not a good idea. A large gate spanned the driveway and a smaller one was at the walk to the house. A large front porch was a further barrier to the massive oak front door. There was no doorbell so Farrell pounded on the door with his fist. It was several minutes before Graciella opened it.

The housekeeper was a short, frail woman with stringy black hair streaked with gray. Farrell guessed she was in her sixties, and she was slightly stooped over. He figured she did minimal cleaning, and the deep lines in her face and protruding bags under her eyes were indicative of a life of hardship and perhaps disappointment. "Mr. Hollingsworth," her voice was weak and unsteady, "I was expecting you."

"May I come in?"

"Surely." She led him to the living room, a room with too much furniture and far too many pictures on the walls. "Can I get you a glass of iced tea?"

"No, thanks. Just some conversation."

"I won't lie to you. Mr. Mauer was an awful man. I have been here over twenty years, and it has been a terrible life and an unhappy house. When Mrs. Mauer was here, he would beat her for no reason and yell at her for the smallest things. When she left, he would curse and mumble like a crazy man."

"Did you get along with her?"

"She was as pitiful as him."

"What do you mean?"

"She let him do all that to her. She should have walked out on him the first time he lifted a fist to her. She should have killed him."

"Do you think she did it now?"

"Maybe, but she is weak, and if she did it now she is dumb."

"Why is that?"

"What good does it do her now?"

"Maybe, to finally erase a bad memory."

Graciella sneered. "You're not too wise for an old geezer. You can never make a bad memory go away. It haunts you forever."

"How do you know that?"

"I lived with the Mister for over twenty years. Even though he is dead, he is still here. Always will be."

"Did he yell at you or beat you?"

"He knew better than to do that. I would have killed him."

"Did you?"

"No."

"Why did you stay?"

"I have no place to go. It is a nice house. He said it would be mine after he died."

"That's motive enough to see him dead."

"Probably so. I may have wanted it, even wished it, but I would not do such a thing."

"Why?"

"Killing is a sin."

"Who else might have wanted him dead?"

She grinned showing poor, yellowed teeth. "Many would not talk to him. Few came here, and if they did they did not stay long. I spend much time in my room and did not care to know details."

"Where did Mr. Mauer keep his papers?"

"In his desk in his bedroom."

"May I look at them?"

"Of course." She led him to the bedroom. "I'll be in the kitchen."

"Thank you."

Farrell spent a good hour going through papers strewn across the top of the desk and stuffed haphazardly in the drawers. Mauer may have been a shrewd business man, and he evidently made money being involved in real estate investments throughout the region and in giving high interest loans to people in the town, but he was a poor accountant and record keeper. Scribbled notes and cryptic descriptions were his main form of noting things, and many of these probably only he could decipher.

Farrell went to the kitchen. Graciella was sitting in a chair smoking a cigarette. "Graciella, I may want to look at the desk again. Please don't touch anything or let anyone else look at them."

"Fine by me."

"One more question. Who was the last person to visit him?"

"Mrs. Rhinegold."

"When was that?"

"The day before he was killed."

FIVE

Over the years when he was a homicide detective, Farrell formulated an investigatory method he called right sight. It was a composite of hindsight, foresight, and insight. Depending on the facts and circumstances of the case he was working on, the ratio of each component would emerge along the way. He could not remember an instance when it was equal parts of each aspect, and it often varied during the conduct of the case. After all, there were cases that lasted for many months, even years, and the longer the case the more adjustments had to be made along the way. Even though the current situation was at an early stage, using the right sight technique offered a scenario that so far there were more possibilities than probabilities. Since Mauer's business connections and dealings stretched well beyond the town, the initial theory that the killer was someone in the town might be off the mark. Persons he may have met with elsewhere could theoretically have been involved, an idea not as remote as first considered. Farrell would still proceed with the assumption that the murder was local as that was so much more manageable, and if that proved untenable then he would branch out. Either way, he was not pleased being so involved. It promised to be a long investigation. He already knew it was a difficult one.

On the next day, he continued with the questioning of those on the list. He would have to wait until the evening to talk with

Peter Clausen because he worked the day shift at the box factory, as well as Grace Ballantree who worked at an insurance office also in Barrington. It looked like it was going to be a long day, the kind of day an old man should avoid if he could. His options, unfortunately, were in reality nonexistent.

Farrell went to Town Hall to speak with Maxine Rhinegold, the Town Clerk and the only town employee other than the Mayor. Maxine was the only person there, and he was hoping she would be totally candid.

Her desk was in an open alcove and she looked up at him as he approached. Rolly polly came to mind as he gazed upon her. She was short and rotund, dirty blond hair was cut short with bangs down to her glasses. She was probably in her thirties. "Farrell," her voice deep and resonant, "Good to see you, even if it is not on town business."

"Ah, but it is. It is the town's business through me to find a murderer on the loose."

"I don't envy you."

"I don't envy me either. Mind if I ask you a few questions?"

She grinned. "Do I need to have a lawyer with me?"

"Not if you are forthright."

"I'll try."

"Good. I understand there was some friction between you and Julius Mauer."

"Not personally, although I couldn't stand him as a person. Some people are naturally grating, and he certainly was one of those. He misused the town by representing he had the Town's authority in his business dealings when he certainly did not, and he would represent that he was acting on behalf of the town which was never true. I would get telephone calls from a host of strangers seeking to verify his credentials and the statements he made. Frustrating and down right dishonest, I say."

"Appalling enough to get him killed?" He sat in the chair across from her.

A moment passed before she responded, and he figured she was searching for the words to sound as neutral as she could. "I wouldn't know why he was killed, although I can understand a number of reasons for it. Some people are so irritating when they try to be someone who they are not or to claim to act for others who know nothing of the matter."

"Do you think anyone in town did it?"

She looked down for a second and then stared into his eyes. "I don't know. It would not surprise me. No one liked him. He ran against Henry Denton for Mayor about a dozen years ago, as you may recall. He received only one vote, and that was his own I am sure."

"Did he have any particular enemies?"

Again, she hesitated. "He treated the whole town as his enemy. You can take it from there."

"I understand you went to his house the day before he was killed?"

"Graciella told you that, didn't she?"

"She did."

"Well, actually, I went to see her, and I had no idea Julius was there at the time. I didn't speak to him and he did not speak to me."

"Why did you go to see Graciella?"

"I don't think it matters, really. She knits, and I wanted her to knit a scarf for me to give my husband for his birthday."

"You could have called her."

"I suppose so, but I wanted to show her what I wanted."

"And, did she say she would do it?"

"Do what?"

"Murder Mauer."

"Very funny. You are barking up the wrong tree here."

"What do you think of Graciella as a person?"

"Have not thought of her like that. Just her being with Mauer makes her crazy in my eyes, and I think she is that way anyway. That house is evil. I get the chills each time I go there?"

"Have you been there often?"

Her response was emphatic. "No."

Farrell then went to the house of David Steele, Mauer's next door neighbor. Probably because of the proximity of age, Farrell had talked at some length over the years with David. David was the oldest resident of Braxton, with Phyliss Braxton second, and Farrell third. He was born and raised in Braxton, and made no bones about saying he never went far away or had any desire to go anywhere. He had never married and was a perfectionist. That is why he had a series of disputes with his neighbor Julius Mauer. He did not like many of the things Mauer did with his property, and was of the mind that some of those things were done purposefully to annoy him. David did not hold back and would forcefully lambast Mauer over such actions. Supposedly, that is one of the reasons Mauer put up an unnecessarily high and strong fence. Another unknown about David Steele was how he supported himself. He had never worked. Horton at one time told Farrell he believed Steele had received a large life insurance bequest from his father when he died. That was, however, over forty years ago.

As a product of his perfectionism, David Steele's house was neat and clean. The house looked like it had been painted recently, and the lawn and shrubbery were manicured with care. Inside was the same when David let Farrell in. Each piece of furniture seemed to be in its rightful place, and there was no clutter, dust, or dirt anywhere. David ushered him in to the living room. "Can I get you some coffee?" David's deep voice matched his tall and husky frame capped by a thick head of gray hair.

"Only if it is already made. Don't trouble yourself."

"It is." He went to the kitchen and came out with a mug. "Do you need anything in it?"

"I take it black. When I was a policeman in New York City I learned to drink it black because there seemed never to be extra time to doctor it up. You have a lovely home. I should have come at earlier times when you invited me."

"Probably so. We might have had some more worthwhile conversations between a couple of old men. I guess you are here now for a different purpose." He sat in the arm chair along side the sofa on which Farrell was sitting, "Of course, from my point of view the death of a despicable person does not warrant the bother of a solution."

Farrell took a couple of sips of the coffee saying to himself that Ava could take a lesson from this man on how to make a good cup of coffee. "Be that as it may. It is something I am committed to solve. Is there anything you can tell me that might be helpful?"

"It's no secret I hated the man, but the line in front of me is long enough. He was the kind of person you expected bad things from. He twisted facts to support his contentions, and his agenda was solely for himself. You just knew you could not trust what he was saying or doing. I'll be honest with you, I'm glad he is gone. I won't miss him."

"Did you kill him?"

David paused for a moment. "Sure would have liked to, and glad someone else saved me the effort."

"If you didn't, who might that someone be?"

"Take your pick. I told you the hate line was long."

"Who might be at the head of the line?"

"The whole town."

"Do you know anything about his business dealings?"

"He made exorbitant loans to desperate people in town. I think he did real estate investments elsewhere, but that is all I know."

"Did you see any strangers come to his house?"

David was silent for a moment, and Farrell was not sure why. "I don't spy on people. Over the years I have seen some cars there that I didn't recognize but was not curious about it. For all I know, they were visitors for Graciella."

"Did you ever speak to his wife?"

"Rarely saw her. I suppose he confined her to the house."

"Have you ever thought of moving so you would not have had him as a neighbor?"

He grinned. "You can't avoid people in a small town. Even if I was not adjacent to him, he would have found ways to annoy me."

Farrell drained the coffee mug, and as he stood he handed it to David. "You and I are contemporaries. There is a special bond that comes with that. I do hope that if you know anything else or find out about anything, you will tell me."

"If you told me you were looking for the murderer to give him a medal, you bet. But, I secretly don't care to be involved in a situation when my heart is not in it. Old age has that kind of prerogative."

"Not for an old policeman."

"You have my sympathy."

It was early afternoon by the time he arrived at Jane Morgan's cottage on the lake. It was just a short way down from his own cottage, within easy walking distance. He parked the car at home and walked from there hoping some fresh air would aid in the thinking process for this increasingly complicated case with no viable leads so far. The walk to and back did not help. Jane was not at home and her car was not in the driveway. He would have to catch up with her later.

Farrell sat in the rocker on the porch, and in spite of the mass of disjointed and interlocking thoughts about the investigation, he dozed off right away. Even sleep could not dispel the overall feeling that he was not getting anywhere.

SIX

Where dreams end and reality begins, or where reality ends and dreams begin matters little in a memory the soul wants to hold on to. It had been thirty-eight years since Beverly died, but it might just as well have been thirty-eight minutes for the gripping emotions that held him captive. When she entered his life he was no longer the same, and when she left his life he was again no longer the same. The window of time they were together was the only truly meaningful portion of his life. It still permeated each breath he took.

That first day when they met, she wanted to see his apartment. After downing the hot dog, they held hands walking to the apartment. A one room apartment might not impress most people, but Beverly was not most people. She loved it. She hugged him and exclaimed, "I want to be here with you!"

He mumbled, "Are you sure?"

"Far, I want my life to be your life. I hope you feel the same way."

"Yes, I do. I am not sure I understand it, and I certainly could not be able to explain it, but I do know this is exactly what I want."

"My dear, Far, we live for us and not for others."

The next day she arrived with all of her possessions – two paper bags filled with clothing. She hugged him as if her body could meld with his, and she hugged him the same way when he left for his shift. She had gone off to recite her poetry, returning using the key to the apartment he had given her. She prepared a meal for them upon his return from what she could find in the refrigerator and cabinets. Thereafter, she was always there whenever he returned from his shift, even after he was promoted to detective in the Homicide Bureau and the working hours were less definite. In fact, she was not only there whenever he returned, she was always there for him with a steadfast devotion and loyalty that to this day he could scarcely believe that she loved him with the kind of strength that defied the frailness of her body. She was unable to have children, and for seven years declined his earnest desire and oft repeated request to marry him so that he could either find another woman who could give him a family or he was totally committed that it would just be the two of them. When they moved to a larger apartment so that he would have space to work on building miniature houses when he became interested in that after they had attended an exhibition and there was the discovery that he had talent in that activity, only then did she agree to marry him. Of course, their spirits had been married from the first day, and the City Hall wedding was just a formality. He knew then that she could be entitled to any of the benefits if he had been killed in the line of duty.

Beverly never gave up on her poetry, and only her love for him was stronger than that passion. Whenever he could, he went with her for sessions when she recited her creations. On their first wedding anniversary he had a book printed of the poems he collected from the pads she used. She cried for an hour after opening up the gift. That book now lay on the small table next to the clock by the bed, along with the poem that she wrote to him just before her death. How she had been able to do that in her fading condition was more of a mystery than the murder of Julius Mauer. He cringed and the ache in his heart escalated as he thought back on that tragedy so personal to him of the debilitating illness and her dying in his arms.

To My Darling, Far –

Do not be sad for me, do not weep,
My short life has been full and complete
Because I have known a love only angels can keep;
I have held my Far in body, mind, and spirit deep.

I am not leaving you, you will not be alone,
I will always be with you in a loving home;
Wherever you go, whatever you do and start,
I will be by your side and in your heart.

My Precious Far, I will love you from afar – forever!

The tears swelled in his eyes and cascaded down his cheeks. An old man can certainly cry when he can remember with clarity a joy or a sadness felt to his core. Even an abundance of years cannot detract from that. She was right. Every moment he sensed her by his side and in his heart.

❖

SEVEN

It was late afternoon when Farrell walked to Jane Morgan's cottage. The car was in the driveway. Before he reached the entrance his cell phone rang, startling him. "Hello."

"Farrell, this is Phyliss Braxton."

"What can I do for you?"

"It is what I can do for you. Can you come for lunch tomorrow?"

"Sure, what time?"

"Is one o'clock good for you?"

"Yes."

"Do you like steak medallions?"

"Whatever that is will be fine. I'm an old cop and just about eat everything."

"Done."

His impression about her wanting to talk with him without Felipe being present was near the mark. Perhaps, he had not lost all of his detective instincts after all. Right sight was waiting in the wings.

Since Jane Morgan was a neighbor, he had seen her now and then and there was always an exchange of pleasantries. He knew she had been married to Mauer and they were divorced. He did not know any of the details of the marriage or its termination and had not heard the story that she had been abused. All of his time in Braxton he tried not only to mind his own business but actually preferred it that way. Knowledge of situations brings a form of involvement, and he wanted to remain as private and uninvolved as possible. Of course, that was not possible now. There was no choice but to look beyond the front doors of homes.

He figured Jane Morgan to be in her late forties. She was not especially attractive, and her broad shoulders on a medium body frame gave the impression of awkwardness. Long straight black hair surrounded a narrow and somewhat elongated face with a wide nose. Her voice was shaking when she opened the door and saw Farrell standing there. "Come in. I knew you would be here at some point."

"Thanks."

She ushered him into the living room. The cottages were similar in size and layout, and he did know she was renting it furnished so the furnishings would not be any indication of the person she was. She motioned for him to sit on the sofa and then sat next to him. "I'm not going to be much help," the voice tinged with slight trembling, without him saying anything. He assumed she was nervous.

"You might be surprised. Tell me about Julius."

"I have not had anything to do with him since the divorce. That was over nine years ago. Before that, life with him was difficult. He was a hard man to please."

"How long were you married?"

"A little over four years."

"How did you meet him?"

"I worked at one of the banks in Barrington. Each time he came in, he made sure I was the teller that served him. I was naive, I suppose, and he made pleasant conversation, so when he asked me out I accepted. I had not dated much. Men did not fall over themselves to be with me. Shortly after that, he proposed and promised me an easy and rich life. I have no family except for a sister in Chicago, and just the day-to-day was a struggle. I wasn't sure I was doing the right thing, although I figured it was an answer to my problems. It sure turned out not to be the right thing."

"Was he ever nasty with others?"

She hesitated for a moment. "I tried not to get involved, but when people came to the house to borrow money from him, sometimes I overheard the conversation, especially when he raised his voice. He was blunt and belittling."

"Jane, I don't want to bring up any unpleasant memories, and you need not give any details, but I understand he beat you."

"That is true. In exchange for me not to press any criminal charges against him, my lawyer at the time was able to get him to agree to a divorce settlement."

"Favorable for you, I presume."

"He had to pay the rent for this place and a monthly allowance."

"Does all that end with his death?"

"I am not sure. The lawyer I had back then has since died. I went today to see a new lawyer in Barrington. He said after reading the papers that it did not look good but it was worth a try to make a claim against the estate."

The right sight kicked in. Mauer's death certainly worked to Jane's financial detriment, but Farrell had seen it before. An emotional trauma could provoke an act of violence even if there might be a substantial downside to it. Of course, if Jane wanted to kill Julius because of the mistreatment she probably would have done it long before this. Yet, the festering process can be long. Perhaps, as Graciella said, a bad memory is forever. "Are you upset that he is dead?"

She answered quickly, maybe a bit too quickly. "No. I am upset that things may become more difficult for me again. I am still trying to put my life back together. It is a long process, and there are times I am not sure I will totally succeed."

"I am sorry, really. You understand that I need to cover everything in the search for a killer."

"I suppose." Her voice trailed off as if she was going to add something but thinking better of it did not.

"How did you get along with Graciella?"

"She was there but not there. Not that I really expected her to help me, but she never even said a word to me even when she saw my bruises."

"Is there anyone you can think of who would gain by his death?"

"I have kept a good distance from anything concerning him. I wouldn't know."

He stood and shook her hand. "I'll try not to bother you again. However, I do have to ask outright. Did you kill him?"

She took a step backwards. "Only in my dreams."

Peter Chaussen lived with his wife, Pat, in a small, ill-kept house just off the main street through town. Their large German Shepard dog barked when he knocked on the front door. Pat opened the door. She was about fifty, graying hair, and slightly chubby. "Farrell, isn't it? We never met, but with any small town I know who you are and probably why you are here. Come in. We are about to have supper. Will you join us?"

"Nice of you, but I have a busy schedule. I won't keep you long. Just a few basic questions."

Peter came over as Farrell entered the meagerly furnished home and shook hands with him. Peter was a short middle-aged man, also slightly chubby, nearly bald and had glasses with thick lenses. "We'll hold off eating until you have done your duty."

"Thanks."

They all just stood inside the doorway, a subtle message to Farrell that they expected the session to be brief. Farrell cleared his throat. "Do either of you know anything about the killing?" They both shook their heads. "Know anybody who might be involved?"

Peter chuckled. "The entire town did not like him."

"I understand you owed him money?"

Farrell was not sure if it was a sneer or a grimace that appeared on Peter's face. "He's our local loan shark. The box company insurance only paid for part of Pat's operation and then my car died. Julius was the only person who could help me out. I have been repaying him but it has not been easy. His death solved nothing. The loan was made through a corporation he set up for making loans and the obligation is ongoing."

"Are you sorry he is dead?"

"No," Peter exclaimed loudly. "I just feel sorry for the town. We have gone from quiet and obscure to everybody's gossip."

"Please contact me if you think of anything else." He had an uneasy feeling as they closed the door behind him. As with the other people he had already talked to, there was the inkling that they knew more than they revealed.

Farrell could see why Mauer had a romantic interest in Grace Ballantree. She was a very pretty and petite woman with a full figure. She lived in a small apartment above a vacant store on the main street. The stairs up to the apartment were shaky, and he climbed them with care. She answered his knock quickly. "Hello, Mr. Hollingsworth," a warm smile rounding out a most appealing woman. "People said you have been questioning folks, so I knew you would get here soon enough. Please, come in."

"Thank you. Please call me Farrell. No sense for

formalities."

She showed him to an arm chair in the living room, a small and neat room with simple furnishings. "May I get you a glass of iced tea?"

"No, thanks. I know you have just gotten home from work so I won't keep you long."

Her voice had a melodic tone to it, nearly captivating in a similar way to Beverly's voice. "That's alright. I am unwinding from a stressful day. I should move to Barrington to be closer to the office, but there are too many memories here. Did you know Jessie before he was killed in the accident?"

"No. I am sorry you lost him. My wife died many years ago although I still refuse to fully accept it."

"So sorry. Jessie and I always admired your houses whenever we went into Horton's store. In fact, Jessie said a couple of times if we ever had any extra money he would love to buy one of them."

"That's nice to know." He felt badly having to change the subject as he could hardly remember how long it had been since he had a form of pleasant conversation. "Let me get to the point so I can let you unwind in peace. Do you know anything about the murder of Julius Mauer?"

"The whole town knows he was interested in me, as well as I had no interest in him. He tried to entice me with promises of money and an easy life of luxury, but I did not like him. I was a bit scared of him. People told me he had beaten his wife, and such an involvement would be the last thing I might be interested in."

"I hate to ask so bluntly, but since you did not want him to bother you, did you kill him?"

She smiled nearly cunningly as close as he could interpret it. "My denials to him and ignoring him put him in his place. If Jessie were here, believe me there would not have been any problem."

"Could anyone else have acted for Jessie?"

"No one can take Jessie's place."

EIGHT

Promptly at one o'clock, Farrell rang the bell at the door to the palatial Braxton home. A thought flashed through his mind that at some point he might build a miniature replica of Braxton Manor, pillars and all.

The maid took him to what he guessed was a sitting room and said that Miss Braxton would be there shortly. He sat on an unusually shaped chair with velvet covering. A chair had a single purpose no matter its shape or how fancy it was. Beverly would have had a good laugh about it, and probably would have written "An Ode to a Weird Chair."

Phyllis Braxton entered the room dressed immaculately in a gray pants suit. Maybe, Farrell thought to himself that she does not wear dresses. She extended a hand to him and grasped his hand firmly. A strong hand shake from a confident woman. "Welcome, Farrell."

"Good to see you Miss Braxton, and thanks for inviting me."

"Call me Phyliss, please. We are contemporaries in more ways than one."

He was not sure about the full ramifications of what she said. "Alright."

"Are you hungry?"

"At our age, I am not sure hunger exists in the normal sense.

I like food, and as a former policeman I can eat at any time and appreciate whatever I get."

"Good. It is a warm day. I thought we would eat out on the veranda."

"Fine by me."

A round glass table with two chairs was set up on the veranda. It overlooked the gardens, and some early spring flowers added a touch of color to the extensive greenery. He knew little about flowers, although that did not detract from his enjoyment of seeing them. He would often give Beverly a bunch of flowers from a flower cart down the street, and she would squeal with delight each and every time as if it was the first time she had ever been given flowers. The little girl in the woman gave him two people to love.

Especially for an old man long accustomed to simple foods, it was a meal to be remembered. Steak medallions were surrounded by puffed potatoes and grilled asparagus, along with stuffed mushrooms. A small salad with fresh greens and strawberries accompanied the main dish. Homemade cheesecake was the dessert. The rich do have access to the finer things of life, and for an instant Farrell wondered what it would have been like if he had gained wealth. For sure, Beverly would have given it away, probably first to every Bohemian poet. All through the meal the casual conversation was pleasant. Phyliss briefed him on the family history and the story of the early glory of Braxton Manor.

After the maid cleared the last of the dishes, Phyliss suggested they take a walk through the gardens. After a few steps, she turned to him and the eyebrows raised. "Let's talk about the murder."

He was not as surprised as she probably thought he might be. "Alright."

They resumed walking. The tone of her voice was emphatic.

If nothing else, Phyliss Braxton was a highly expressive person. "Any suspects yet?"

"There seem to be a whole bunch of people with a motive. Determining inclination is much more difficult. Julius Mauer was an unpopular man."

She chuckled. "That's a fact. And so will you, Farrell, if you continue with your investigation."

"I am not expecting to win a popularity contest. I'm just doing what has to be done."

"Let me explain what the heart of the situation is. We don't know each other very well, so let me tell you I do not mince words. I also don't want to sound boastful, but the truth sometimes makes it so. This is my town; these are my people. Family history and tradition compels me to look out for them, to protect them and the town. They are like lost sheep. They look to me to guide them. This Mauer situation has them in panic mode. Many feel their lives are crumbling around them. The town and a good number of the people are dependent on the activity and income from the summer residents. Memorial Day is six weeks away, and that is the official start of the summer leases. There have been two cancellations already. The word is out that because of the murder Braxton is unsafe. I need for you to wind this up quickly before it goes from bad to worse." She glanced sideways inviting his response.

"I am doing all I can? What more can you expect?"

She put her hand on his arm. He was not sure if it was a menacing maneuver or one to add emphasis to what she was about to say. "I would like you to exonerate the town."

He had also stopped walking and faced her fully. He looked directly into her blue eyes, and in a way it reminded him of the many times he had gazed into Beverly's wide brown eyes in an attempt to see the inner workings of an active and imaginative mind. He hoped his voice sounded stronger to her than it did to him. "I can't do that unless and until it works out that way."

"I am not asking you to give up the investigation. All you have to do is to indicate it looks now like the murder took place away from the town with no involvement by any of the people in the town. The only connection with Braxton is that the victim was a resident and the body was dumped here. No local persons are prime suspects, and there are increasing clues that a person or persons Mauer may have had business dealings elsewhere may have committed the crime."

"I don't have any such clues."

"But, it is possible. If that becomes the main premise the heat on the town is off. If later on it turns out to be a town person, that will be as a less damaging afterthought."

They resumed walking and had reached the outer limits of the gardens so they started back to the house. "You think it was a person in town, don't you?"

She smiled, and even a smile through aged cracked lips can be mischievous. "Murder is so far removed from this sleepy old town that I think if it actually was here it would pop right up and bite you on the hand."

He was not really sure what she meant by that. "And, you think it was a woman?"

"As an old man you know better than to try and analyze the mind of an old woman."

"If you tell me everything you know, I am sure there will be a quicker resolution to all of this."

That smile again. There is a fine line between mischievous and cunning. "Farrell, I have told you all I know and all that I expect from you." They had reached the veranda. "You must come for lunch again."

He knows when he has been dismissed. He shook her hand, her grip firm as a recapitulation of the request of him, thanked her and left. He had been a detective long enough, as well as a keen observer of human nature, to conclude that she had not told him everything she knew. Adding to the dilemma of solving the crime was whether to heed the directive of Braxton's queen. This was his home, and this was his future as limited as that might be. If she was inclined to and malevolent enough, she could make things difficult for him. You cannot escape from reality as it goes wherever you go.

NINE

The autopsy report was a shocker! The cause of death was not from the knife. It was asphyxiation. Since there were no marks on the neck, strangulation was unlikely. Suffocation would seem to be the primary possibility. The knife was inserted into Mauer's back after he was dead.

Right sight propelled a further scenario. It would now seem most likely that the killing did not occur at the lake. If the killing happened elsewhere, why was the body taken to the lake where it was bound to be discovered? Thick woods located north and south of the town might have delayed or even prevented discovery of the body. The killer apparently wanted the body to be found. Why? Was it a message of some sort? If the killer was from the town, the worst place with respect to damaging the reputation of the town was to have the body found within the town limits. Who, where, or when the knife was inserted was a complicating unknown.

Farrell had given much thought to Phyliss' request. It was not as outlandish as his first reaction to it. It would not sway him from the course of the investigation even if the outside world thought otherwise. He was propelled into a decision to accommodate Phyliss' wish when a reporter from the newspaper in Barrington contacted him about the autopsy. Whatever he responded to that would probably be picked up by other newspapers in the State and beyond. He informed the reporter in as general terms as he could that initial indications were that persons beyond Braxton might be involved and the investigation was trending that way. Perhaps, for the moment everyone was satisfied except Farrell.

Mayor Denton's reaction to the autopsy was one of disbelief. He asked Farrell to meet him at The Cup and Saucer. He was sitting at the counter when Farrell arrived. Ava was the only other person there, and the grin on her face indicated she believed she would be privy to some good information to tell others.

Farrell sat on the stool next to the Mayor, waving off Ava's offer for some coffee. The Mayor's face was stern. "Well, where do we go from here, Chief Law Enforcer?"

Farrell tried to put a positive spin on it. "We know that there is most likely one or more people besides the killer that had contact with Mauer before the body was moved to the lake."

"Despite your newspaper interview, it still looks bad for the town. If it wasn't for the knife, maybe we could have called it a suicide. By the way, can whoever did the knife thing also be a murderer?"

Farrell noticed Ava edging closer to them. She did not want to miss a word. "No, you can't kill something that is already dead. Desecration of a dead body, maybe. It might help if we get a forensic specialist to look into the matter. Tests might be revealing."

"How do we go about doing that?"

"We would have to hire one."

"Forget that. The town has no money for anything like that, which I assume would be quite expensive. You are on your own on this."

"Probaby would be, although we could get lucky and catch a killer."

"What next?"

Farrell knew, but he was not going to let Ava know. "Not sure. I'll keep going. If you think of anyone I should talk to besides those on the list I showed you, be sure to let me know."

He knew exactly where he was going. He was on his way to Mauer's house to look again at his desk and papers when the cell phone rang. "Hello."

"Hello, Farrell, Phyliss here."

"I recognize your voice."

"Just wanted to thank you for what you told the newspaper."

"It does not change anything. I'm still doing what I am doing."

"I expect so. Yet, just maybe, all will come together."

"Is that a riddle?"

"A prediction."

"Based on what?"

"Enjoyed your visit. Bye."

It took Graciella a couple of minutes to respond to his knock on the massive door. "I was in the back," was her curt welcome.

"I would like to look through his desk and papers again."

"I haven't touched a thing."

"How come you told me Mrs. Rhinegold was the last person to visit Mr. Mauer? She says she came to see you."

Graciella sneered. "Is that what she told you? She came to see him."

"She said she wanted you to knit a scarf."

"She did ask me that before she left, after she was with the Mister for a good half hour."

"Are you sure?"

Graciella turned to walk away. "You know where the desk is. You believe what you want to believe."

As he made his way to the bedroom, Farrell told himself that he had to talk to Maxine again. Someone was not telling the truth.

Farrell spent more than an hour going through the papers. He made a list of any name he came across with a cross reference to property, monetary amount, or other subject linked to the name if there was such information. He would eventually have to get a warrant to examine the corporation's records if there were any. He had an inkling that there was a corporation in name only and that Mauer was the corporation.

Farrell stopped at the Town Hall to speak to Maxine but the building was closed. He went to her house a few blocks over, a modest frame structure. Maxine's husband, George, answered the doorbell and told Farrell that Maxine had gone to Barrington although he did not know why or when she would be back. Talking to her would have to wait.

When he arrived home, a handwritten note had been slipped under the door.

COME TO THE CLOVERDALE SCENIC OVERLOOK
TOMORROW AT 10:00.

It was not signed and the writing was unfamiliar. "Now what?", he thought to himself.

TEN

After a light supper, Farrell went to the back porch and sat in the rocker in the dark. He stared out into the blackness where the lake was supposed to be. He knew it was there, he just could not see it. It struck him such was the same situation with the murder investigation. Somewhere in the crime darkness were the answers.

He closed his eyes. An escape from the rigor of these full and frustrating days was needed, and there was only one source of mental comfort that might alleviate the agony. Thoughts and the memory of Beverly wedged into his mind temporarily obscuring his unsought involvement in the world of crime.

Beverly was an amazing person. Her sensitivity to life and people was the major component of her caring nature and her desire to please. Her love for him was boundless, and she declared that often verbally and in verse. She adapted her schedule around his commitments so as to be together every possible moment. The sleep schedule was a special adjustment. She would only sleep whenever he did. When he was on a rotating police schedule and had to work the night shift for a week at a time, she stayed awake all night while he was on patrol so she could sleep with him during the day. Her explanation was simple enough. She could only sleep when she was holding him, as holding him was the way she was sure he would not get away from her.

On his days off, they had an assortment of activities they did together, including leisurely walks, going to the repertory theater to see old movies, and trying as many different ethnic foods that they might find. One of their favorite pastimes was going to used bookstores and combing through old poetry books. When Beverly would come across a poem that caught her attention, she would read it aloud to him. They would discuss its meaning, its sincerity. That would usually inspire her, and upon returning home she would curl up next to him on the sofa or in a chair later on if he was working on a miniature house, and a new creation would emerge from the endless fountain of ideas in her mind.

Beverly would experiment in making new food dishes for them to share. Her ingenuity was not confined to verses. They would laugh at culinary failures and cheer at the successes.

Farrell only took a one week vacation in the summers. He was paid for unused vacation time, and the extra money was put to good use. There also might be emergencies, as well as later on when he was in full swing building the miniature house there needed to be time for exhibitions.

For that summer week they had discovered a quaint bed and breakfast country inn near Lenox, Massachusetts, and stayed there each summer. Since they did not have a car they would rent one, and even that was an adventure. That area afforded them many activities for the week. The nearby lake was a total novelty to them. Renting a row boat or canoe gave them hours of a new kind of pleasurable activity together. Because she was so thin, Beverly would not wear a bathing suit. She would not even wear shorts as she exclaimed her skinny legs would scare away birds, fish, and anything else that moved. They would spread out a blanket at Tanglewood and listen to the music under the stars. There would be dance recitals at Jacob's Pillow as well as summer stock theater at Stockbridge. There would be bike rides on a bicycle built for two, and hikes on the easy mountain trails. Beverly was unable to hike very far, and there would be many rest stops. Tiredness set in quickly, and there would be recurring pain in her legs. Her frail condition was always a major concern for him, and there was always the dread of it as a precursor of bad times ahead. None of that would daunt her spirit and enthusiasm, and as long as she had him by her side she proclaimed even if it was an easy trail she could conquer mountains.

Special memories blossomed from those vacations, and pictures in the album were nearly worn out from his fingers turning the pages. The shared closeness ushered in new sensations, new vistas, and new dreams. Her laughter haunted his hearing. Her smile loomed constantly before his eyes. Her kisses were engraved on his lips. One should be grateful for every moment of contentment and pleasure. Once taken away, its absence is an ache in the heart. Any fullness to him as a person was with her and for her. Without her he was a mere shadow drifting in and out of the events and people surrounding him. Alive, but merely going through the motions of living.

ELEVEN

A few minutes before 10:00 o'clock Farrell drove into the Cloverdale Scenic Overlook, the last rest area before the Canadian border. There was only one other car there, an older Ford with a Canadian license plate. He parked in the adjacent spot. Behind the wheel of the Ford was an elderly looking man with straggly gray hair and beard. The man motioned for Farrell to get in his car besides him. As Farrell got out of his car, he placed his hand over his jacket assured that the gun was snug in the shoulder holster.

When he sat next to the man, he noticed he was short and that a cane was resting next to his seat. The man smiled, revealing a broken tooth in the front of his mouth surrounded by yellowing teeth. His voice was unsteady, and that could have been from old age, an infirmity, nerves, or all of the above. "My name, Mr. Hollingsworth, is Pablo Avello. I am Graciella Avello's older brother."

Farrell thought he better say something to put the man at ease. "I didn't know Graciella had any relatives here."

He shook Farrell's outstretched hand. "I used to live in Braxton. I moved to Canada, probably a few years before you moved there. I did not like the attitude of the people there towards Hispanics. They think all we are good for is menial labor. The United States Government is not much better. That is why I moved to Canada. I am in a Canadian Government run retirement village now."

Farrell hoped his impatience did not show itself too much. "Why did you want to see me?"

"There is something you need to know."

"What is that?"

"My sister and me have always been very close. When I was in Braxton she arranged for me to do odd jobs for Mr. Mauer, and a couple of times he did not pay me because he did not like what I did. The man was real mean."

"You are not telling me something I don't already know."

"That is not what I want to tell you."

"Alright."

"One night, a long time ago, I happened to pull in right here one night to have a cigarette. There was just one other car there, and I could see that it was a young couple necking. They did not see me as they were so involved in what they were doing, but I recognized the car and the boy and girl. It was David Steele and Phyliss Braxton. They were secret sweethearts in high school. They have been very careful and secretive. They are still lovers today."

Farrell could not hide his surprise. "How do you now that?"

"Graciella sees and hears everything. My sister shares information with me. What she knows I know. Miss Braxton visits Mr. Steele in the middle of the night."

"She could have told me this."

"She didn't think you would believe her. People say some wrong things about her, particularly that she is losing her mind. There is nothing wrong with her at all. She wanted to make sure you heard it directly from me. We have never told anyone else about this, and even in a small town there can be secrets, important secrets."

"Why are you telling me?"

"Graciella and me think they killed Mr. Mauer."

Farrell gulped and for an instant could not find his voice. "Why do you think that?"

"Mr. Steele hates Mr. Mauer. Miss Braxton thinks Mr. Mauer is ruining the town. We think too that somehow he found out about the two of them and started blackmailing them."

"Do you have any proof they killed him?"

"That's for you to do. It's your job. Not going to be easy. I am an old man as you are. We have experienced the unexplainable. Sometimes you can't prove what everybody knows."

"Talking riddles doesn't help prove someone committed a crime. I can't understand the blackmail angle. Why would they care really if everyone found out they are in love? Neither is married, and it is nothing to be ashamed about."

"If you ever get to know Miss Braxton you will find out she wants everyone to know she is perfect and in a class by herself."

"Why do you think they never got married? Seems to me that would have been acceptable."

"Two very independent people can love each other but they probably cannot live together. That is what Graciella thinks."

"I appreciate you telling me all of this. Is there anything else, no matter how small, you know that would help?"

"No, just a warning. Miss Braxton is a powerful woman. I wouldn't put anything past her to do if she feels she needs to do it. If she knew me and Graciella knew about them, we would be dead by now. Don't you say where or how you found all of this out. You be careful, very careful."

"I always am."

TWELVE

While driving back to town, Farrell had much to sort out in his mind. Right sight would hopefully enable him to keep it orderly. First, how credible was Pablo? Without any proof, how could Farrell even begin to confront Phyliss and David with an accusation that they murdered Mauer? It would be highly unlikely that they would confess to such a deed. How certain could he be that Pablo's claim that they were sweethearts and lovers was even true? It was just his word, perhaps bolstered by what Graciella might believe without actually knowing for sure. Further, by Pablo's own admission he moved from Braxton because of the Town's attitude toward Hispanics. The town is Phyliss, so Pablo has a grudge against her. Stirring up the pot might be his way of getting revenge. Second, even if they are lovers, why would Phyliss and David murder Mauer? There is no proof of him blackmailing them, and even if that was true Phyliss surely has the money to keep him quiet. Surely, some other scheme short of murder could have been devised to drive him out of town. A powerful woman potentially has many means at her disposal to get what she wants. Then there is the sticking point, even if they were involved, why the placing of the body by the lake? Perhaps, an equally forceful assertion could be made that Graciella and Pablo committed the murder and implicating Phyliss and David is a way of deflecting suspicion away from them. Graciella was tired of catering to a mean man and wanted the house while she was still able to enjoy it. Pablo also had a grudge against Mauer for bad treatment and nonpayment of some things he did for the man. Yet, because of their age and physical conditions, how could they overpower Mauer or even dump the body by the lake? The image of Graciella stooped over and the cane by Pablo's side emerged. There was also the mysterious aspect of who or why the knife in the back. Of course, it very well might be somebody else entirely. It is often said that the truth is elusive. Especially is this so in the realm of crimes where facts may be difficult to decipher, participants wary and secretive, and interpretations can vary widely.

Another factor loomed large. Once the summer residents arrived, the increase in the number of people actively around would make the investigation even more difficult. There had been no further cancellations. The pressure was building for him to solve this, and in spite of tenuous suspicions he was not sure he was anywhere close to solving this baffling case.

He decided he would stop to see Maxine and then go talk to Graciella to try and pinpoint more of what she knew or thinks she knows. Then, he would go to talk to David Steele to find out his shoe size and just maybe something pointed would slip out during the discussion. The cast of the footprint at the lake was a man's size 10.

Maxine did not seem overjoyed to see him. "More questions?", was her curt greeting.

"Sorry, but I have to get to the bottom of this. Graciella says you went to see Mauer and spent time with him before talking with her."

"Well, she's mistaken, and I think she is not all there, if you know what I mean. As I told you before, Mauer was there, but I

64   RIGHT SIGHT

did not talk to him or spend any time with him."

"Anything else you might have thought of since we talked before."

Her response was quick and emphatic. "No."

"Alright, thanks. I may be back."

She muttered, thinking perhaps he could not hear her. "I can't imagine why."

Again, it took Graciella a few minutes after he pounded on the door for her to open it. "I knew you would be back."

"You also know why I am back."

"Come to the kitchen and get your questions over with."

He followed her through the house to the kitchen in the back. He noted her stooped over condition, shuffling of feet, and it would seem unlikely she could lift a body even with Pablo's help. In the kitchen, she motioned for him to sit in a low back wooden chair that was next to a small table. She leaned against the sink facing him directly. He might as well start with the biggie. "Did you see them kill him?"

She shrugged her shoulders. "No."

"Then how do you know they did it?"

"Figures."

"Explain that to me."

"It reached the boiling point. They had enough trying to deal with him in any other way."

"I don't see that. Convince me."

"It's the way I figure it. If it doesn't work for you, you figure something else out."

"I can't accuse somebody of something based on speculation."

"Makes sense to me. That's all I need."

"Alright, let's approach this a different way. How do you

know Miss Braxton visits Mr. Steele at night?"

"I've seen her come. My bedroom faces his house."

"How often?"

"Once or twice a week."

"What time?"

"Around 2:00."

"Aren't you asleep then?"

"My arthritis keeps me awake most of the time. I doze on and off. Her car makes noise when it goes on his gravel driveway."

"How long does she stay?"

"Varies. Sometimes an hour, sometimes two."

"There is nothing I found in Mr. Mauer's papers that would indicate he was blackmailing them."

"The man, as hateful as he was, was no fool. If I knew, he eventually found out. He would roam around the house at all hours of the night."

"Doing what?"

"Your guess is as good as mine."

"Why didn't you go to Canada with Pablo?"

"And do what? Mr. Mauer was no good but it was a job and I hoped the house would be mine some day."

"Were you impatient for that day to come?"

She did not answer right away. He sensed she was as cunning as he surmised her to be. "Figuring it that way is all wrong."

"I am not so sure."

"Play with a snake and it may bite you."

"You and I are not finished."

"You know all I know. What you do with it is your snake."

As Farrell closed the gate behind him, he looked over and saw David Steele outside of his house trimming a bush. It was too good an opportunity to pass up. He also noted the gravel driveway.

David looked up as Farrell approached. "Been talking to Graciella?"

Farrell added, "And going through Mauer's papers. Nothing specific, but there are indications he may have been blackmailing some people."

David stopped the trimming and stood up erect. "Doesn't surprise me. Anything bad about him is believable."

Farrell did not detect any change in his stance or expression. "How well do you know Graciella?"

"We go back a lot of years. She has seen many bad things in that house. If I heard all the yelling at Jane and the screams when he beat her, you can imagine what she heard and saw."

"Have you gotten along with her?"

"She has always been respectful and I stay out of her way."

"Do you know she has a brother, Pablo?"

"Yeah. He used to work here and moved to Canada a long time ago. Haven't seen him since."

"What is she like as a person?"

He paused for a moment. "Never quite looked at her that way. I don't think she is well and aging quickly, perhaps even getting senile, but she doesn't cause me any problems."

"Do you think she might be capable of murder?"

He paused again. "Don't know. Don't care to know."

"Probably most people are capable of murder."

He stared at Farrell before he spoke in a monotone. "Don't know. Don't care to know."

"Thanks." Farrell started to walk away and then turned back. "One more thing. What is your shoe size?"

"11 ½ D. Why do you want to know?"

"I ask everyone that. There is a footprint by the lake."

"What size?"

"Not your size."

THIRTEEN

It was easy to check the high school records as they had all been digitized. Phyliss Braxton and David Steele were students there at the same time. Of course, that did not prove anything about a relationship, if any. It seemed strange to Farrell that the Braxton family would send a daughter to a public high school, but that was beyond the scope of the investigation. Yet, curiosity can be limitless and strong at any age. He would wait a week, and if no other leads opened up he would seek to talk again with Phyliss.

Farrell went to the Braxton Post Office, a tiny store that could barely accommodate more than three people at a time, and talked with the Post Master, Thelma McGuire. Mauer went there from time to time, although she never had any extended conversation with him and noted he was often rude. Ned Harris, the sole postal carrier for Braxton, was also of no help. He could not recall anything out of the ordinary on the route around the time of the murder, and he had never had any face-to-face dealings with Mauer.

Farrell then conferred again with Horton and Greta about who else he might talk with who had loans with Mauer or possibly some dispute. It was time and energy consuming meeting with the ones they came up with, and it added little new information. All disliked the man for his actions and attitude, particularly his lack of any concern or sympathy for individual hardships. All were shocked by the murder and disavowed any knowledge of or participation in the deed. All were dismayed at the tarnished image of the town and feared that any future prosperity was in jeopardy. Farrell even had the sense that some now even harbored a form of personal resentment towards him and his involvement in trying to seek a murderer among the people of the town.

Whenever he could, he sat in the rocker gazing out over the lake. It had a calming effect on him, and he was able to quiet his frustration a little. The mist on the lake early in the morning took on a new symbolism. To see the water clearly, the mist had to be lifted. For him to gain right sight over the homicide, he had to discard irrelevant notions. There were just too many pieces to this puzzle to fit together to get a clear picture. To develop an investigatory strategy at this point was also troubling. After retiring, he thought he would never have to face such dilemmas again. Beverly often told him that there was no such thing as never, and there was also no such thing as always except for their love.

Farrell watched as bands of rain moved across the lake. Beverly loved it when they walked in the rain. She liked the sound of the drops on the umbrella, and she would proclaim that it soothed her soul so she could write better poetry. What she especially liked was the excuse, as if she really needed one, to clutch herself to his side so the umbrella covered them both. She also liked the rain when they were on the summer vacation at the Inn. It had a tin roof, so the sound of the rain was quite pronounced. She would describe it as Nature's orchestra playing a romantic symphony just for them.

FOURTEEN

Farrell was planning to call Phyliss and ask her if he could come over to discuss some matters with her. He would start off by informing her that he would like to do a miniature of Braxton Manor and get her permission to do so. Then, perhaps, other topics might come up in discussion and something might slip out. Before he could call, she called him inviting him for lunch again. That meant, he was sure, that she also had some matter she wanted to discuss with him.

There would be no dining on the veranda or walk in the gardens this time because on the day of the lunch a cold pounding rain descended on Braxton. It seemed odd to him for a setting of two at the exceptionally long table in the large dining room, although he surmised that such was not only acceptable among the rich it was also coveted. From his early pronouncement of eating anything, she did not tell him the menu beforehand, but it was once again memorable for an old man with limited fancy culinary exposure. Shrimp cocktail was followed by a fresh green salad with chunks of roasted salmon in it and then crème brulee. He could get used to this but definitely did not want to.

Phyliss was dressed in a light brown pants suit and her gray hair was neatly placed in a bun on the top of her head. It accentuated her clear complexion. She was a well preserved and interesting woman for her age, and he guessed she was quite a beauty when younger. It made it easy to understand why David may have been attracted to her early on and explain a continuing fascination.

"I was thinking," Farrell broke a temporary silence, "That once this case is over I would, with your permission, like to build a miniature of Braxton Manor."

She smiled. "That would be fine. I have admired your talent in Horton's store. I am sure it would be magnificent and I would purchase it from you. I can imagine placing it in a special setting in any number of places in the house."

"Last time, you kindly gave me a history of the Manor and the family. You never mentioned anything about your personal history."

"There is not much to tell. What would you like to know?"

"Did you always plan to live here?"

"I do my duty. The Braxton tradition is compelling. There was a time, however, I thought I might become a fashion designer. After graduating from an elite all girl's college, I studied at The School of Design in New York City."

Farrell wondered if doing a duty included eliminating threats. "Why did you give it up?"

"My father died and there was no one else to run Braxton Manor. You may not know, I have a younger brother. He works for the General Accounting Office in Washington. He lives there with his wife and two sons. The Braxton name will live on. I am hoping one of the boys will take my place here when I depart this world."

"I hope you don't mind me asking, why did you never marry?"

"Not an interesting story. I suppose I had my share of suitors, but they were all more interested in my money than in me."

"Did you go to an exclusive high school?"

A momentary hesitation was revealing. "No, I actually went to the public high school in Barrington."

"How come?"

My father believed at the time that it would sit well with the people of the town. It would show them that we did not think we were any better than they are."

They finished the meal and went into the parlor. Not that he really expected it, but it would have been real friendly if she had asked him some personal questions about his life. The rich can pretend that they are no better than the rest of us, although that does not last long and does not convince many.

Once settled in one of the massive sofas in the parlor, Farrell anticipated the real reason for his invite would emerge. At times, he hits the nail on the head. "I have a favor to ask of you," looking beyond him at one of the portraits of her ancestors hanging on the walls, "And I have no way of saying it except to come right out and say it."

"I don't expect anything else."

"Good. I would like you to drop the investigation. You know better than I do what convincing reasons can be given when a case turns cold. I am sure there were cases you worked on in the city that never got solved. It happens."

She waited for him to say something. "Why do you think the case will go unsolved?"

"From what I see and hear, there are no prime suspects. Nobody cares if it gets solved. A bad man is gone and it is actually a relief. The important thing is that everyone can relax and the town can go back to what it was and what it was meant to be. You can go back to the life you came here to have."

He wanted to shout out that maybe he had prime suspects although proof was lacking, He knew better than to do that. "Yes, I have had my share of cold cases, although a cold case is a thorn in a policeman's side. There is a never ending pain that justice has not been served."

"To me, justice is relative. If no one cares about it, what justice needs to be satisfied?"

"There is the justice of society at large that when a crime is committed the criminal should be found and punished."

"Nice words to support but not necessarily to live by. The way I see it every person in town wanted Mauer gone and death as the end justified the means."

"If we all believed such things, we would be living in a jungle."

"I commend you for your honorable outlook, but we all know, especially at our age, that for every rule there are exceptions or ought to be."

He knew he had said what needed to be said. It was time to move on. "Maybe so, maybe not."

"Dear Farrell, please think about this. I would be most appreciative. Your miniature of Braxton Manor would be a grand acquisition."

The implication was clear enough, and one need not be a detective for it to register. That was the least of his considerations. He had to admit to himself, however, that even if this was a common criminal case it was set in an unusual environment. Where progress ends or should end was now his dilemma. Graciella would probably say that this too was his snake.

FIFTEEN

The summer came and went; the summer residents came and went. Braxton was returned to its sleep mode as the autumn chill set in. Without him doing anything to make it so, the case also turned cold on its own. Whether Phyliss believed Farrell was behind the current status or it just evolved that way was of little difference.

During the summer Farrell made several trips to companies in the region which were noted in Mauer's papers that he had some business dealings with. Each trip turned up nothing except a shared opinion that Mauer made grandiose and often misleading statements, although he had a keen business sense concerning the timing and placing of investments.

Farrell sat in the rocker, his jacket buttoned up and a hat on his head. Fallen leaves were being blown in all directions by a fierce cold wind, many floating on the water. The case had fallen apart. Plenty of people with motives, plenty of opportunities. Not a shred of proof to tie any of it together. It was as if right sight had blinders on.

Old folks pride themselves on their experience, and the often pronounced thought that they have seen it all offers some security against the unexpected happenings of life. Farrell had not only not seen it all, he had probably only seen a small fraction of it. So many cases he had handled in New York City would turn on an unanticipated event that he was still of the mind that there might be a surprise happening to affect the outcome here. It might be months away, or even years, or it might be the next day.

Early on the following afternoon, Ned Harris, the mail carrier, knocked on his door with his mail instead of putting it in the box. "Hey, Mr. Hollingsworth, you said I should let you know if anything out of the ordinary happens. The mail has piled up at the Mauer house for three days. That is very unusual. Graciella promptly gets the mail from the box, and many times she is even waiting out there for me."

"Thanks, Ned, I'll look into it."

Farrell went to the Mauer house, gathered the mail, and proceeded to the front door. When there was no response to his pounding after several minutes, he tried to open the door. It was locked. He went around to the back of the house and found the back door to be unlocked. He opened it and called out for Graciella. When there was no response he went in. He found her in bed dead. There was no sign of foul play. From the stench and her ashen color, he guessed she had been dead for at least two days.

Farrell telephoned the doctor in Barrington who certifies deaths, and he came right out and certified that Graciella had died from natural causes. While Farrell was waiting for the doctor he searched the room. He did not find a will but did find an opened letter from the Canadian Government that read she was being notified as next of kin of the death of Pablo Avello on September 17, cause of death cardiac arrest, and that if the body was not claimed within seven days it would be sent to the Government Crematorium.

Once the doctor left, Farrell called the State Coroner to request a confidential autopsy on the body. He asked that the body be picked up after dark in an unmarked van. Then he called Mayor Denton with a detective's fib that he had found Graciella dead, the doctor had certified that she had died in her sleep from natural causes, and that since Graciella had no known living relatives the body was being sent to the crematorium in Barrington. That would be the story available for public consumption. Mayor Denton then told him something quite interesting. Although Graciella did not have any relatives now that Pablo was also deceased, she did have a very good friend in town, in fact a man who was known to fancy her, Manuel Cortez, the short order cook at The Cup and Saucer.

A week later the confidential autopsy report was received. The cause of death was asphyxiation. Farrell had an inclination that was going to be the result.

Right sight fully kicked in and this is the way Farrell thought it had all played out, perhaps with a nudge or a tweak one way or another. Mauer was blackmailing Phyliss over her relationship with David. She could not tolerate the man or the thought of giving him money. She arranged with David to kill him, making it look like he died from natural causes. David agreed to it because he loved Phyliss, she was supporting him, and he hated Mauer as well. They enlisted Graciella's help, which she readily agreed to because of her greed to get the house. The night before the body was discovered, Graciella let David into the house after Mauer went to sleep. David suffocated him, perhaps with a pillow over his face. The plan was probably for Graciella to call the Mayor the following morning proclaiming she had found the Mister dead in the bed. The Mayor would get the doctor out who would then certify that the death was by natural causes, and everything would be neatly wrapped up. However, at some point after David left the house, Graciella, in a moment of senility or built up detest for the beast of a man that she had to serve for so many years, or both, took a knife from the kitchen and either forgot Mauer was already dead or to make sure he was dead, plunged the knife into his back. Upon realizing what she had done, she wiped her fingerprints from the knife and got Pablo to help her take the body to the lake the following evening. Somehow, they physically managed to do this between the two of them. Or, perhaps, she had gotten Manuel Cortez to help them. Confirmation of that theory came when Manuel Cortez was killed in an automobile accident. Supposedly, he was driving to Barrington, lost control of the car for some unknown reason and struck a tree. Knowing that it would anger Phyliss and David, they had decided to leave the body by the lake thinking that this way it would look like one of Mauer's business associates did it because a town person would not leave the body in the town. They could not predict that Farrell would proceed first with the theory that a person from the town committed the crime. The annoyance Phyliss had for what Graciella had done ripened into anger and rage when Graciella and Pablo decided to blackmail her over the murder convinced that she would not kill again. They woefully underestimated the woman's will. After a reasonable time had passed, action followed. By eliminating the only eye witness and the only other person who knew about it, any possible link or proof was wiped away.

The fly in the ointment was Farrell. Phyliss and David apparently did not know that Graciella and Pablo had told him about the love relationship and had accused them of the murder. Farrell could only assume that he was told all of this as a form of assurance in the event that the whole scenario went sour.

SIXTEEN

It was a bit of a surprise when a week later David invited Farrell over for coffee. He probably should not have been surprised because once he thought about it the more he figured that David and Phyliss would want to tie up any loose ends, one of which would be to find out just how much Farrell knew. Farrell accepted the invitation hoping he might come away from the meeting with some information that might put his theories on firmer ground.

David answered the doorbell right away. He seemed jovial enough. "Glad you could make it."

"Nice of you to have me."

"Come in and a couple of old buzzards can shoot the breeze while we drink coffee and nibble on the oatmeal cookies I made this morning."

"Sounds like something I can handle."

David led him to the kitchen where there was a small table in a breakfast nook. As Farrell would have guessed, the table was neatly set. A carafe of coffee was next to a platter heaped with cookies. "You plan on fattening me up?", Farrell asked lightheartedly.

"The recipe called for two dozen, and I did not want to vary from it. You can take some home with you."

"By the way, how do you stay so fit? I don't eat much but the pounds seem to come by themselves."

David poured the coffee for both of them, and took a bite out of a cookie. "I have exercise equipment in one of the rooms. I work out twice a day."

Farrell ate a cookie and sipped some coffee. "Too ambitious for me. Good coffee, and delicious cookie, David."

"Thanks. What do you do besides building the houses?"

"I meditate. I can sit in the rocker on the back porch for hours, stare at the lake, and my mind takes flight. My favorite time is early in the morning when the mist clings to the lake. It is magical as the mist slowly lifts away, and it inspires me to think long and hard about things."

"What sort of things?"

"Mainly about my wife. She was the love of my life. She has been gone for nearly forty years, but the memories are alive each moment. Have you ever been in love?"

"Sure, in my younger years."

"None stole your heart?"

"There were some possibilities. None fit my expectancies. After awhile, living alone becomes a life style."

"A lonely one?"

"Not really. Besides exercising, I read for long periods of time. The house and yard keep me busy as well."

"Did you have a girl friend in high school?"

David reached for another cookie, and Farrell guessed he was thinking about how truthful he should be. "A couple as best I can remember. Did not amount to anything."

"Did you ever consider a career?"

"I don't have the temperament to work for someone else, and no business idea ever struck my fancy." He hesitated for a moment and Farrell just knew he was going to change the subject. "Are you finished with your investigation?"

"Yes and no."

"Which means what?"

"Yes, in the sense that my prime suspect was Graciella. I had no proof just the feeling an old cop develops. It is baffling how, in her condition, she could do all of it. I guess I'll never know. Yet, there were cases I handled when in New York when I thought I was at a dead end and then something would pop up and a new lead was there to follow. No proof, of course, but it seems logical that someone helped her."

"Maybe, her brother."

"Maybe. He is dead, too, and was in poor physical condition."

"Puzzling, I can see that. We are old enough to know that life deals us situations we can never figure out and probably should just accept without going through any fruitless mental exercise."

"Did Graciella ever ask you for a favor?"

David straightened out in his chair. "What are you getting at?"

"Nothing, just you would have been convenient for her."

Farrell could tell David was a little perturbed. "Well, she didn't, and I wouldn't have anyway."

"Do you know if Graciella knew Miss Braxton at all?"

"I wouldn't know, although I would doubt it. Graciella did not get around much, and I never saw Phyl...., I mean Miss Braxton over this way. Why don't you ask Miss Braxton? Why do you ask that anyway?"

"Just as I have been told by others that if anything needs to be done in terms of the town, they ask Miss Braxton."

"I never heard that. I never asked her for anything."

"How well do you know her?"

A moment's hesitation. "Not all that well. We have talked

upon occasion, although not at any length."

"Have you ever been to Braxton Manor?"

I have been there just about every Christmas when she holds an open house with refreshments for people of the town. I don't recall seeing you there at any of the Christmas celebrations. Have you ever been there?"

"Never did go at Christmas, but she has had me for lunch recently. I think she is trying to find out if I am a good detective."

"Are you?"

"Apparently, not good enough."

They spent another hour in casual conversation, mainly how an elderly person tries to keep up with the fast moving changes in the world around him. When Farrell left, his right sight had been bolstered. He also felt he had conveyed a number of things he hoped David would be satisfied with. He did not know where to go next in the investigation although he was a good enough detective to keep on asking questions, although the interviews with people were merely fishing expeditions.

SEVENTEEN

It was a harsh winter. There was a greater than average snow fall, plenty of ice, and howling frigid winds. For Farrell it was a frustrating winter. There was little rocker time, as well as the near constant wrestling with his conscience. He had a pretty good idea who committed the murders and why, all without any proof and even without a way of making it a convincing possibility in an explanation to anyone, especially to one interested in the town and its future. The boat wreck on the lake presented an added lesson. Once an investigation is abandoned, over time it is destroyed.

The age factor was critical. He was eighty-two, David eighty-seven, and Phyliss eighty-six. How much longer any of them might live was a crucial unknown. When the last of them died, the crimes would be just an historical notation. He thought of making a conclusion in a detailed written report for posterity, but without any proof such a conclusion would be an empty gesture and not convincing. He was at a loss at what to do. As the early signs of spring emerged he decided to do nothing. It would be a wait and see what happens, and it was equally frustrating to realize that did not promise to be productive. The one decision he did make was not to build a miniature of Braxton Manor. He did not want Phyliss to believe that he was conforming to her wants.

Farrell also thought about resigning as Chief Law Enforcer,

although he thought it best to keep the law enforcement authority just in the event an unanticipated development occurred. He also flirted with the idea of moving away as he did not think he would ever be entirely comfortable in Braxton again. Yet, he did want to be here if something did happen because he might be the only one to recognize its significance. Also, it would be a sign of a personal failure if he opted for an escape route. He had been a lost soul since Beverly's death. Now he was also a wandering soul in a vast wasteland of knowing what was right and without the means of doing anything about it. In a way, he died when Beverly died, and now it seemed as if he had died again. How many times can a person die before it is final?

The next day while sitting in the rocker the scheme hatched in his mind. It would be his final death that could bring justice. He would send a letter, one copy to Phyliss and one copy to David. It would describe that on the day Farrell discovered Graciella's body, he had gone to the Mauer house because the mail carrier had indicated the unusual circumstance of the mail not being emptied from the box outside the gate. When he arrived there, he had gathered the mail from the box and put it in the back of his car temporarily. Then he was so involved in finding the body and its aftermath that he forgot about the mail in the back of the car. Just recently, he found it there. In the mail was a letter from Pablo to Graciella. In it was a signed statement by Pablo detailing the role he and Graciella had in the homicide of Julius Mauer, arranged by Phyllis Braxton and carried out by David Steele, as well as the relationship between the two of them. There was a place at the end of the statement for Graciella to sign it too. The accompanying letter indicated that once she signed the statement she should put it in a sealed envelope and give it to Farrell to be opened only upon her death. This would be their safety valve if Phyliss balked at paying the blackmail amount or considered any act of violence against them. Farrell would then advise about the actual autopsy performed on Graciella's body and its obvious implications. The letter would then close with an expectation that they both would confess and turn themselves in to face punishment for their crimes. Copies of Farrell's letter, as well as Pablo's letter and the statement were in the hands of other law enforcement officials, including the FBI, to be opened in the event something happened to Farrell. The FBI would have jurisdiction if a law enforcement officer was killed.

So, there it was. The choice was to either do nothing and await the demise of the three of them so that the crimes would be relegated to a footnote in the history of Braxton, or to force the issue with what for all intents and purposes would be a risky scheme. It was a dangerous chance because the only recourse for Phyliss and David, other than surrendering which was unlikely, would be to kill Farrell and hope he was bluffing.

A week passed and Farrell was still undecided. The easiest decision, and the one with the least ramifications, would be to do nothing. He would be the only one to suffer knowing he was, in effect, assisting criminals to get away from their deeds. He could lose himself in building miniature houses and in the recall of the warm memories of Beverly. Yet, there would probably be moments his pronounced conscience would second guess that decision. He would have to avoid looking at himself in the mirror.

If he sent the letters, the town of Braxton would be adversely impacted. The arrest of the queen of Braxton would mean the end of the Braxton dynasty and its oversight of the town and its inhabitants. The salacious story would most likely receive national coverage. Farrell's remaining days would be, at the very least, uncomfortable, facing the constant scorn from the folks of the town. Not what he wanted then or now. If there was a successful attempt on his life, would that final death be worth it? He would not know the future because he would not be a part of it.

If you were Farrell, what would you do?

POSTSCRIPT

At Christmas, 2042, the festivities at Braxton Manor were as lavish as always. Nearly every town resident showed up for the food and beverages. When Hermle Braxton moved from Washington, D.C. with his wife and their two children to Braxton Manor in 2029 after his Aunt Phyliss died, he made sure all of the old traditions were carried out. This included being the overseer of the town and its people. Hermle made it his top priority that the Braxton name would be forever revered. One of the first things he did was to completely redo the family burial site at the back of the property just beyond the gardens, so that any of the folk from the town could come and tour the site, rest on one of the benches, and reflect on the prosperity the town continued to enjoy as a product of the Braxton Dynasty.

The old story of a murder that had been committed in the town had been told and retold so many times, often embellished with outlandish facts, that many of the younger residents did not believe the event ever really happened. It was cast as a sort of folk tale or a horror story to be told around a campfire.

The one other story that was told in the horror genre was when crazy man David Steele died a year after the passing of Phyliss Braxton. He had been the talk of the town for years as a man overtaken with Alzheimer's and had to be under constant nurse care, and who would shout and curse at people. After his death, the letter found in his nightstand describing his participation with Phyliss Braxton in various murders was dismissed as the product of the disjointed mind of a crazy old man.

Another early action taken by Hermle was to establish an actual two person police force with a police station in a renovated downtown store. That would calm the complaints about travelers speeding through the town on the way to or from Canada. There had been no law enforcement presence in Braxton since the suicide in 2022 of Farrell Hollingsworth who was the Chief Law Enforcer. He had been found drowned in the lake. Since Hollingsworth left no note explaining why he was taking his own life, most were of the opinion that the failure and frustration of not being able to solve the murder eventually proved to be too much for an old man to bear. Support for such a theory came from the smashed miniature houses in his cottage along with a mostly burned up photo album.

The day after the body of Farrell Hollingsworth was pulled from the lake, there was an unusual occurrence at Braxton Lake. A thick mist hovered over a portion of the lake for three straight days. On the day after the mist lifted, a young girl, frail and rather sickly, was walking slowly along the shoreline. Ahead by the old boat wreck which had always fascinated her, she saw a book that had apparently been washed ashore. It was wet although intact. The cover and the pages were legible. The cover read: A Collection of Poems by Beverly Myers. The girl smiled, clutched the book to her chest, and headed home with her treasure.